The Tale of the Castle Mice

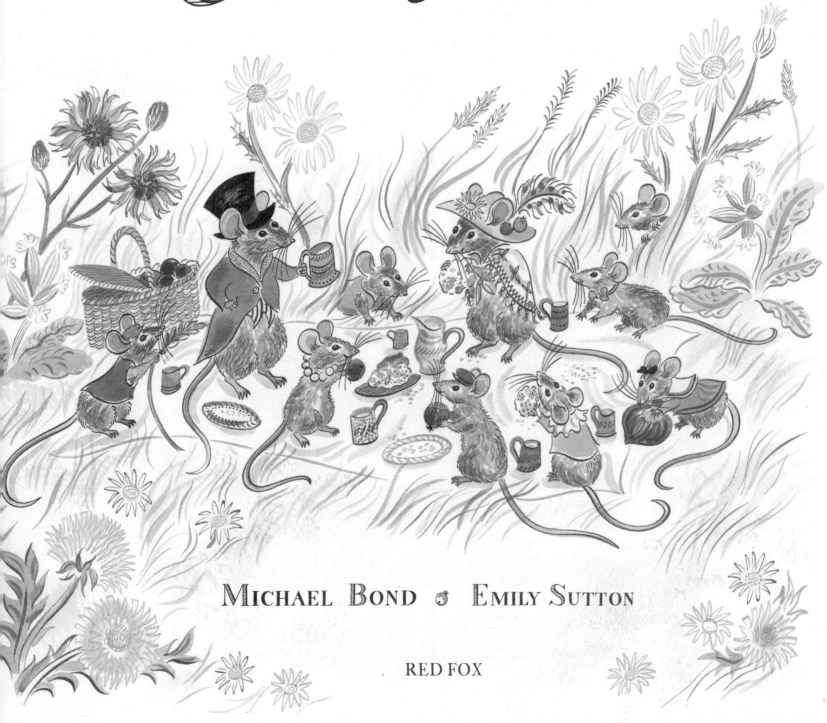

MICHAEL BOND ❧ EMILY SUTTON

RED FOX

The Tale of the Castle Mice

For Josh – M.B.
For Penny – E.S.

RED FOX

UK | USA | Canada | Ireland | Australia
India | New Zealand | South Africa

Red Fox is part of the Penguin Random House
group of companies whose addresses can be found at
global.penguinrandomhouse.com.

www.penguin.co.uk www.puffin.co.uk www.ladybird.co.uk

Penguin
Random House
UK

First published by The Bodley Head 2016
Red Fox edition published 2017
001

Text copyright © Michael Bond, 2016
Illustrations copyright © Emily Sutton, 2016
The moral right of the author and illustrator has been asserted

Printed in China
A CIP catalogue record for this book is available from the British Library

ISBN: 978–1–782–95401–9

All correspondence to:
Red Fox, Penguin Random House Children's,
80 Strand, London WC2R ORL

ONCE UPON A TIME there was a family of mice
who lived in a doll's house. There were fifteen of them:
Mr and Mrs Perk and their thirteen children.

Their house was owned by a rich earl who lived in a castle, and apart from having one wall missing it was very grand.

There were two bathrooms, both with running water.

Mr Perk slept in the
larger of the two baths

and his wife occupied
the other.

The children made do on shelves
in one or other of the many rooms.

Being unusually large, the doll's house was full of nooks and crannies and could have taken many more children. But Mrs Perk decided to stop at thirteen.

"Enough is enough," she said.

The Perks rose early every morning and

polished
the silver,

shook the rugs,

and swept up
after themselves.

Afterwards, when lots of visitors came to visit the castle, they disappeared through holes in the wainscoting and there wasn't one to be seen.

All the visitors to the castle said it was the best-kept doll's house they had ever come across, and many of them took photographs of it.

Mrs Perk was a good cook and she kept a well-stocked larder of leftovers from the castle kitchen, so the mice never went to bed without supper. One way and another they lived a happy and carefree life.

During the long summer evenings they played games on the castle lawn . . .

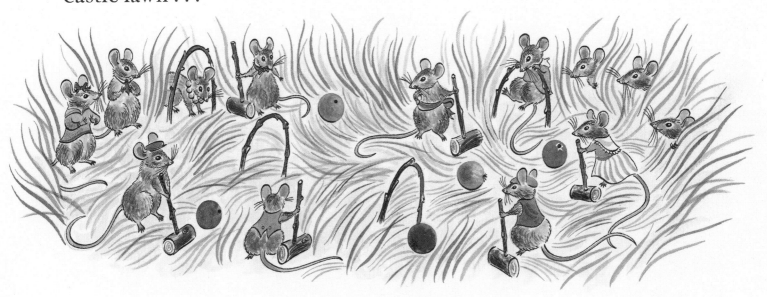

and in the winter, when it was cold outside, they sat in the lounge and watched television by moonlight. It was a very tiny screen and the picture never changed, but it helped pass the time.

Then one day something happened that threatened to change everything. The family woke to a strange smell.

"It's paint," said Mr Perk, who knew about these things. "They must be decorating the castle!" And sure enough, when they looked outside there were ladders everywhere.

But there was worse to come.

As the days passed and the castle grew more and more inviting, their doll's house began to look so down at heel, no one bothered to take pictures of it any more. It was even suggested that they should do away with it altogether.

"But they can't do that, Dad," said Mrs Perk. "Can they?"
"Believe me, Ma," said Mr Perk gloomily, "there's no such word as 'can't'."

That evening Mr and Mrs Perk went for a walk. While they were out, one of the children had an idea.
"We must 'do-it-ourselves'," she said. "Get scrubbing, everybody!"

They found some washing-up liquid, and in no time at all there were bubbles everywhere. In fact, there were so many bubbles, they soon lost sight of each other.

To make matters worse, the paper came away from the walls and soon there were great piles of it everywhere.

As it dried out, the glue set hard, trapping some of the smaller Perks, who began to cry.

The sound of their sobbing brought Mr and Mrs Perk running, and when they saw the state their house was in, they could hardly believe their eyes.

"What are we going to do, Ma?" asked Mr Perk. "If you ask me, it's a right old mess."

"They meant well, Dad," said Mrs Perk, "so we can't really be cross. But, oh dear. Oh dear. I don't know what the earl will say when he sees it."

She didn't have long to wait. The very next morning the earl took one look at the doll's house and ordered it to be removed. "Goodness me!" cried Mrs Perk. "I never thought I would live to see our home being taken away on a lorry."

"We shall have to look for other accommodation," said Mr Perk.
"I'd sooner have somewhere to live," said his wife.

But with winter coming on it wasn't easy to find anywhere, and in the end they had to make do with a garden shed belonging to the castle.

Christmas was a very sorry affair. Food was scarce,
nobody had any presents, and they had to pile on top
of each other to keep warm.

Then, one day in early spring when they were beginning to think they would never, ever, be happy again, the mice heard the sound of cheering and clapping coming from the castle.
"Hush, everyone," called Mrs Perk.

"By popular request," said the earl as the first visitors arrived, "the doll's house has been restored by some of the best craftsmen in the country. I wouldn't mind living there myself instead of in this great castle," he added amid laughter, as everyone rushed to take pictures.

That night the Perks moved back into their old home and held a Grand Opening Party of their own. Mrs Perk made a cake and there were seven different kinds of cheese.

"Just think, Dad," she said when it was all over and the children had gone to bed. "They may be small, but if they hadn't made such a mess of trying to help, this would never have happened."

"Good things often come in small parcels, Ma," said Mr Perk. "And if you ask me, the earl needs us as much as we need him. I think it's high time we went to bed too."

"Lights out, everyone!" he called.

Soon there wasn't a single snore to be heard.

The Perks were all as quiet as only
a happy mouse could be.